D1569046

AFRICAN WRITERS SERIES
Editorial Adviser · Chinua Achebe

52

The Afersata

AFRICAN WRITERS SERIES

The Afersata

B. M. SAHLE SELLASSIE

HEINEMANN
LONDON NAIROBI IBADAN

In memory of my father

Heinemann Educational Books Ltd
48 Charles Street, London W1X 8AH
PMB 5205 Ibadan · POB 25080 Nairobi

EDINBURGH   MELBOURNE   TORONTO
SINGAPORE   HONG KONG   AUCKLAND

ISBN 0 435 90052 8

First published in African Writers Series 1969
Reprinted 1970
Printed in Malta
by St Paul's Press Ltd

1 *Fire in A Village*

The night Namaga's hut burnt down all the inhabitants of the thirty villages of Wudma were sound
asleep. So were their cows, their zebus, their
donkeys, their goats and their chickens. This
happened a little before cockcrow at the time of
the night when the field cockroaches were silently
resting under the dry branches of fallen trees; when
the country frogs and toads were hiding away in
their stagnant pools; when the hyenas were roving
the villages searching for dead bodies, and howling
and calling each other to share their prey; when

the river snakes, according to children's tales, were feeding on the shimmering stars, their tails attached to hedges and their heads reaching out towards the heavens; when the village thieves were active digging under the leaves of the mud-huts; and when criminals were killing their own kind and looting their properties.

The night Namaga's hut burnt down every male adult woke up from sleep at the resounding shout of 'help!', and rushed out of his shelter and ran to the blazing fire, 'leaving his pants behind' as the saying goes, in order to put out the roaring fire. Some arrived carrying water in big jars and in small jars; others came panting, carrying water in big gourds and in small gourds; still others cut the green leaves of the enseta plants and flung them on the roof of the burning hut; the rest of them dashed into the hut and carried out boxes, stools, sacks full of coffee beans, clothes, and materials that were dear to replace.

Namaga's hut could not be rescued. The fire was too powerful to fight back. There would have been some hope of extinguishing the raging fire if the incident had happened in the month of July when the earth is but a stretch of black jelly and the sky a black mass of clouds that turns into hail, and comes down like millions of pebbles thrown down by millions of devils. But this happened at the end of May, and not in July, just before the first showers of the cold rainy season started to fall, at the time of the year when the countryside was all yellow and dry. Even the rivers, except the biggest one that flowed throughout the year and from which the villagers and their livestock quenched their thirst, except that big river, all the rest were dry, and their beds were covered with yellow leaves and dry grass.

The thatched roof of Namaga's hut smoked, sagged and crumbled down. The leaves that made up the circular wall emitted red and blue flames, glowed and broke down to the ground. Every piece that was part of Namaga's hut except the central pillar turned into ashes.

The outer layer of the central pillar turned into charcoal, but the inner part remained untouched. The pillar stood erect as if it were planted there by some devil right after the destruction of the hut. And Namaga, as well as the other villagers was happy that the central pillar was still upright, for that foretold that the criminal who set the hut alight would be caught. Indeed, according to the traditional belief of the country folks, the fate of such a criminal always lay in the position of the central pillar.

The villagers knew that the criminal was hiding somewhere in the enseta plantation, and that he was watching his fate. They knew that he would not run away before he witnessed the fall of the central pillar.

When the hut was totally destroyed they decided to hunt the criminal. They divided into four groups and dispersed in the four directions of the earth.

Some entered the bushiest part of the enseta plantation crushing the dry weeds under their bare feet. Others went as far as the coffee plantation that stretched further away from enseta plants. They searched the criminal until dawn and returned home with sleepy eyes, exhausted and totally dismayed.

The villagers who did not come at night to help put out the fire, that is, elders who lacked strength to run for help, and others like the Cheka Shum (a minor official) whose position relieved them of the obligation to take an active part in such unhappy events, all such people came in the morning to see Namaga and to console him for the loss.

When the Cheka Shum arrived Namaga was sitting in his other hut which he formerly left for his cattle and for his tenant, Aga. At the sight of the Cheka Shum Namaga rose from his jute mat and stepped outside.

'May God replace your hut with a better one,' said the Cheka Shum examining the remains of the hut. The corpse of a rooster was lying in the middle of the ashes. All its feathers were gone and its open beak was filled with grey ashes. The Cheka Shum, holding his nose between his forefinger and his thumb to prevent the bad smell from entering his nostrils, turned the corpse with the tip of his shoe and said again, 'May God replace your hut with a better one.'

'Amen,' answered Namaga in a morose tone.

[4]

'We shall investigate the whole matter soon. These days our villages are deprived of peace. It's not even a month since Beshir's uncle lost his goats. There are criminals and thieves in our villages, and we shall dig them out wherever they are,' added the Cheka Shum.

The inhabitants of the thirty villages of Wudma had no police force to investigate crimes. But they had their own method of going about the matter. When the Cheka Shum said, 'we shall investigate the matter,' he meant what he said. Although his primary function was to collect the land tax and the tithe for the government his authority went much further than that. The Cheka Shum was all at once a judge, an executive officer and a tax collector.

In most parts of Ethiopia the office of the Cheka Shum has always been hereditary, and his influence on all matters connected with the villages paramount. Contrary to the general rule, Argaw, the Cheka Shum of the thirty villages of Wudma, had acquired his office by dynamic personality and not by heredity. He was not even a native of any of the thirty villages of Wudma.

In twenty years the mystery surrounding the origin of Argaw has never been solved. According to his own version of the story he was the grandson of a high government official who served his country as governor of a certain region in Shoa during the reign of Menelik II. His father, again according to his own version, had been a major in the Imperial Army and had died in action during the Italian invasion.

The villagers, however, accepted the story only as a half truth. They did not contest the fact that his grandfather was under the service of Emperor Menelik II. But they did contest the part of the story that tried to make them believe that his grandfather was a governor of a certain region. Instead, they were convinced that his grandfather was the head servant in the royal palace, a position which was not in fact much inferior to that of a governor of a small region. It is also very possible that Argaw's grandfather was initially a head servant in the royal palace, and that he was later appointed governor of a region as a reward for his loyalty to the Emperor.

As for his father there was no doubt about his occupation. Many villagers who knew him in person confessed that he was an ordinary soldier, and not a major in the Imperial Army, who met his death on the battlefield.

As the pursuits of Argaw's forefathers, during the fascist occupation, were wrapped up in doubts, so was the role Argaw played. He was at that time a young man of twenty-two. He told the villagers a thousand times that he was a patriot, and that he had joined the guerillas led by Ras Ababe and had killed at least fifteen fascist soldiers. The inhabitants of the thirty villages of Wudma, however, strongly held the opinion that he was a renegade who had sold the freedom of his country for Italian spaghetti.

Whichever was the true story what matters to us now is Argaw's position as a Cheka Shum. The Cheka Shum has always been the lowest official in the administrative structure of local government. Above him there is a sub-district governor and below him the tenant farmers who are popularly known as the rural people.

During the last twenty years Argaw never complained of not being promoted to a higher status, or of not being paid a regular monthly salary like other government officials. The world was divided into two distinct groups, in his opinion – those who governed and those who were governed – and as he belonged to the governing class, it did not really matter much whether he was at the bottom of the administrative structure or a little higher up. He was in fact proud of holding the position of a Cheka Shum for twenty solid years, during which time many officials had been transferred to other regions, or had lost their position altogether.

In a land where illiteracy is the rule rather than the exception, in a place where the slightest sign of education is an article of admiration, to be a Cheka Shum, and especially a literate Cheka Shum, is indeed something great. And Argaw was one.

'Are you intending to bring the matter of your hut to the attention of the governor?' he asked Namaga, intentionally goading him in that direction.

'Yes, sir, if you will help me to do so.'

'Then bring a sheet of paper this afternoon to my house and I will write you a report to the governor. Now I must go to the court as I have an important matter to settle,' said the Cheka Shum and left.

A long, thin stick in one hand and a sheet of lined folio paper in the other, Namaga set out for the village of the Cheka Shum. It was early afternoon. The blue sky was veiled, at various points, with patches of white clouds which shaped themselves now into animal figures, now into human forms, and now into giant monsters, and finally disappeared into nothingness to reappear, once again, in other forms. The black shadows of eucalyptus trees which lined the dusty path leading to the village of the Cheka Shum stretched out and contracted as the trees swayed regularly with the wind. Namaga walked on the grass. The dusty path was too hot for his bare feet. He walked fast leaning on his stick, and wondering how much the Cheka Shum would charge him for writing the report to the sub-district governor.

Argaw did not have any fixed price for writing reports for the villagers. The amount depended entirely on him. He sometimes accepted a bottle of intoxicating liquor produced locally, and known as *arake*. Every important person in the countryside drinks *arake*. A man who drinks much liquor without getting drunk is considered to be virile. And officials like the Cheka Shum could empty half a bottle of highly intoxicating, dry *arake* at

[8]

one sitting and still be able to walk without faltering. For them drinking is a hobby.

In the villages like those of Wudma there are no bars. But some of the village women brew local beer, mead and *arake* in their spare time. The stronger the liquor they brew the more they are appreciated. If no liquor is available in the villages then the official would have his mule saddled and would ride to the town where the sub-district court is located and have his fill there. Or he would simply ask a young man from the village to go and get it for him from the town. It is rare, however, that the officials spend money from their own pockets to buy liquor. They get it free of charge from those who have some pending cases to be settled.

The Cheka Shum was sometimes satisfied with a chicken or fifty cents cash to write the report. And if the tenant farmer offered his service to the Cheka Shum during planting, weeding, or harvesting seasons the Cheka Shum would even write such reports 'free of charge'.

The inhabitants of the thirty villages of Wudma always preferred to have their reports written by Argaw, although they had other alternatives. The village schoolchildren, for instance, could do it as well. But the tenant farmers were never sure whether the young students had such beautiful handwriting as the Cheka Shum. His calligraphy was special and everybody in the village talked about it. He took the greatest pain lest he should cross out any word or leave any dirty mark on the white paper. He even used blotting paper despite the fact that he rarely wrote his reports in ink. Besides, the sub-district officials were particular about the language used in such reports. The sentences had to be long and the vocabulary well selected so that the matter really appeared serious and demanded great consideration. Moreover the heading had to be accurate. If the heading was inaccurate the report would be rejected, in which case the tenant farmer would incur more expenses by buying another sheet of lined folio paper for five cents and going back to a professional report writer. Another cause of rejection was the illegibility of the report. The young school boys who were taught not only Amharic but also English were so used to attaching one letter to another in their writings that one could hardly read what they wrote in Amharic. Amharic letters forming words stand separately from each other as in typed English words and each word is separated from another by a colon. But the school children were so used to the foreign way of writing that the officials in the sub-district office could hardly read anything written by them. For all these reasons the villagers, including Namaga himself always preferred to confide their reports to a professional hand, that of the Cheka Shum.

Namaga arrived at the gate of Argaw's compound which was enclosed by a rectangular fence made of upright beams interlaced with the thorny branches of the acacia tree. In the large compound a sheep, probably brought as a bribe by some unfortunate tenant, was tethered to the fence. The grey mule of the Cheka Shum was also grazing nearby. The compound contained two huts, a big one for servants and cattle, and a small one that the Cheka Shum used as his office, bedroom, and guest house, all at once.

Namaga heard strange and familiar voices as he approached the small hut. Only on rare occasions was the residence of the Cheka Shum empty of people. Creditors came to sue their debtors who refused to pay back what they owed. Tenant farmers whose crops had been destroyed by the cattle of their neighbours came to accuse the owners of the cattle and to receive compensation for their loss. As the Cheka Shum was one of the people closest to the sub-district governor, at least in his office, favour-seekers came requesting that the Cheka Shum introduce them to the sub-district governor. The age-old institution known as *dedje tenat* or asking for favour, an institution that has benumbed the creative spirit of the people, has always been common not only in higher circles but also in the lower echelons. The institution of *dedje tenat* calls for loyalty on the part of the favour-seeker and benevolence on the part of the giver. So as a result a person's sense of achievement and reward, as well as his initiative and his creative spirit are crushed.

Namaga placed his stick against the outside wall

of the smaller hut, among the canes and sticks of those who were inside, and after arranging his cotton toga properly he bowed at the entrance of the hut which was packed with people.

'You came a bit too early,' Argaw said to him, although he had not given him a fixed time to come. When they met that morning Argaw told him simply to come in the afternoon which meant any time between noon and six o'clock. 'Take a seat and wait. I must settle first things first,' went on Argaw. He was indeed busy. All those round-headed peasants did not come to his residence simply to see his face. Each had a problem of his own.

After about three hours had elapsed the Cheka Shum turned his eyes to Namaga to tell him that it was now his turn.

'I brought one sheet of paper,' said Namaga, unfolding the roll and presenting it to Argaw. The white paper had turned a little brown in the middle where Namaga had been holding it. It also smelt of fresh sweat.

'It is sufficient,' answered Argaw and pulled out a blue ballpoint from the outer pocket of his khaki coat. He had in the chest pocket of his coat three ballpoints that appeared to have been stuck in there more for prestige than for use. Ballpoints, fountain pens and pencils are symbols of literacy, and some people stick them in the most visible part of their clothes as if they were medals of honour.

Argaw picked up a copy-book from the floor,

placed it on his crossed thighs, and stretching out the folio paper on the copy-book started writing.

To: Ato Gabre Mariam Belachew
    Governor, the sub-district of Wudma
    Chebo and Gurage Region
    Dear Sir:

I, Namaga Buta, the reporter, wish to bring the matter of the burning of my hut to your kind attention.

On the eve of Tuesday, May 17, 19 . . , just before cockcrow, an unknown criminal set my hut alight, thus destroying part of my property, and attempting to murder me and my family. Thanks to the prompt action of my neighbours as well as of my fellow villagers, part of my property was rescued from a catastrophe. But despite all our efforts to put out the fire my hut burnt down to ashes, and consequently I lost, among other things that will be specified later on by word of mouth, two hundred dollars in cash and ten quintals of coffee grains that I preserved for future unforeseen circumstances.

Dear Sir:

As you are the guardian of poor folks and the wiper of their tears, as you are also the arch-enemy of thieves and criminals I beg you, falling under your feet and kissing them, to have the crime investigated, and to bring down the criminal to his knees.

[13]

Hoping that our gracious God will aid you in your noble task, I remain your obedient servant,

Namaga Buta.

When the Cheka Shum finished writing the report he read it aloud so that everybody could hear it. 'What do you think of the wording of the report?' he asked, addressing nobody in particular.

'It's perfect,' said one fellow.

'The governor will be deeply moved,' said another.

'Nothing more could be added to it,' said Namaga himself.

'Then come and sign it,' said the Cheka Shum.

Namaga was illiterate like almost all the village folks, and did not know how to sign. So instead he wetted the tip of his forefinger with his saliva and offered it to the Cheka Shum who instantly marked it with a copying pencil. Namaga then placed his fingerprint at the bottom of the page, and the Cheka Shum wrote Namaga's name once again round the fingerprint.

Two days later the sub-district governor ordered the Cheka Shum to convene the people for the Afersata, a meeting of the villagers, to investigate the crime.

The inhabitants of the thirty villages of Wudma hated the Afersata. They hated it because they were under an obligation each and all of them to attend it. Whether the villager had a previous engagement or not, whether he had urgent work on hand or not, whether it was harvest time or planting season, he had to go to the Afersata. It was a rendezvous from which, in the expression of the villagers themselves, 'no one could stay away even at the cost of leaving the dead unburied'.

Formerly only members of the high village society attended the Afersata. Now, however, every male adult including those who once formed the submerged class, that is wood-workers, leather-workers and blacksmiths were obliged to come to the gathering. After all they could very well be murderers and criminals like every one else!

Despite the inconveniences created by the Afersata, members of the submerged class considered it a privilege to attend the meeting. As far as they were concerned it was a new step towards the recognition of their civil status. Formerly they were outcasts who lived on the fringe of village society because of the trade they practised. As wood-workers, leather-workers and metal-workers they were despised and pushed aside from all social and civil activities.

If the Ethiopian peasants could not improve their material life over the centuries it was probably because they could not enjoy fully the fruits of their labour; and if material progress stagnated it was probably because the creators of material civilization were despised. The man who carved wood, the man who tanned leather and the blacksmith who forged iron into utensils was an inferior creature by the fallacious logic of the ignorant.

Argaw the Cheka Shum fixed a date for the Afersata, and passed the order to the villagers through his thirty assistants. His assistants whom we may call the village headmen were not government employees. They were elected by the villagers themselves and acted as sort of errand boys to the Cheka Shum. They went from hearth to hearth and informed the villagers of the date and place of the Afersata. They also assisted the Cheka Shum during the collection of the various types of taxes. As a reward they were exempted from paying land tax on the plot of land they cultivated. In this respect they resembled a bit the Cheka Shum himself who although a government employee, had no monthly salary. His annual payment consisted of the land tax collected from one gasha, forty hectares, of land.

The place of the Afersata was fixed to be in the central village called Kafa. It was chosen because it was central and no-one would have to walk for more than two hours to get there. Besides that advantage a huge oak tree offering shade throughout the day stood in the vast meadow of that village, where the livestock were driven to graze. It was under that leafy oak tree that cattle tenders sat to play the flute and to eat wild date palms and that the village children made fires to roast the green corn-cobs they had stolen from prohibited farms. Yellow birds had built thousands of nests in its branches, and black ants inhabited its hollow trunk and roots.

Adults avoided the oak tree only when it was raining. Children were warned not to approach it even when the sky was cloudy, for it attracted the 'Boje' the spirit of the sky that appeared in the form of a golden axe and caused a blow of death.

During the dry season, however, there was no danger of the spirit of the sky, and as the oak tree offered a cool shade the Cheka Shum decided to make it the place for the Afersata.

A few villagers gathered at Namaga's hut over a kettle of coffee before the hour of the Afersata. There was first of all Aga, a fellow whom we have introduced as Namaga's tenant. In actual fact Aga was a sub-tenant, for Namaga himself was a tenant of an absentee landlord, and by pure logic Aga, Namaga's tenant, was the sub-tenant of the absentee landlord. Aga cultivated part of Namaga's plot and gave him in return one half of whatever he produced, and kept the village cattle when it was Namaga's turn to tend them. The sub-tenant's wife was also there, an active woman who gave assistance to Namaga's wife whenever the occasion demanded it. There were three other neighbours and their wives who were invited for morning coffee as was customarily done.

The sub-tenant was sitting on a low stool by the fireside warming his bare legs. His shorts were so wide and loose that one could see his thighs almost up to his private parts.

'Put more faggots on the fire, woman,' he addressed his wife, scratching his leg.

'You think perhaps that the faggots come by themselves from the woods!' she answered in a half questioning, half exclamatory tone, 'we have no more faggots, and remove your feet from the fire-place,' she added.

The sub-tenant's wife never respected her husband, and he knew it. But still he would never dare divorce her, because first of all she was a distant relative of Namaga, and secondly because if he did he would never find as suitable a wife as she.

The sub-tenant was a huge, strong man, but his brain was just the opposite of his body. He lacked the ability to think. In fact if it were not for the proper guidance of his wife he would be no better than a child. If she let him do as he wished he would step out of his hut and start amusing himself with insects as the village children do. She had indeed to be a martyr to live with him as his wife. 'That's my share,' she said when people suggested that she should run away from him and marry a more sensible person. 'It is my lot. I cannot help it. God wished it to be that way and I must live up to it.'

The sub-tenant was a stupid fellow as everyone in the village knew. But, on the other hand, he was an indefatigable farm hand. He would work for hours on end pulling out weeds or splitting wood or ploughing the field without as much as ten minutes rest. He worked like the devil and ate like a cow. Namaga liked him particularly for his hard-working spirit, for when Namaga went to the sub-district court simply to listen and enjoy the arguments between the accuser and the accused, their dramatic gestures and their high sounding words, or when he went to attend a funeral, the sub-tenant worked on both Namaga's and his own plot.

'Remove your feet from the fire-place,' said the sub-tenant's wife, addressing her husband, 'you always seem to shiver like the village goats in the rainy season,' she added.

'You mean I am a goat?' asked the sub-tenant, in a foolish tone that made everybody present laugh.

The calves mooed in the stable part of the hut. They were begging to be let loose and to suck their mothers' udders. The youngest calf that was born a month ago sucked all the milk from its mother's udder despite the protest of Namaga's wife who wished the mother cow to be milked. Namaga loved his cows and calves. He never allowed a cow to be milked until its young was at least two months old, and even then the cow would be milked only partly. He considered it unjust to deprive the young ones of their mothers' milk at an early age.

The cows lowed in answer to their calves' moo-ing. 'I suppose it's time to drive the cattle to the meadow,' said Namaga without addressing anyone in particular.

'They are not yet milked,' answered his wife.

'Remove your legs from the fire-place, and go and milk the cows,' the sub-tenant's wife ordered her husband.

The poor husband rose up from his stool, rolled his toga-like shemma into a ball, and putting it on his stool went in the direction of the stable, naked above his waist. He let one calf loose, and waited for a while until the calf wetted its mother's udder and made it ready to give its milk. Then the sub-tenant pulled away the calf, dragging it by its hind leg, and tied its lower jaw with a rope, the other end of which he fastened to the central pillar of the hut. Then holding a black, clay container he squatted to milk the cow. But the cow kicked as there was a slight scratch on one of its nipples. The sub-tenant fortunately drew back his hand just in time, otherwise he would have broken a finger. He stood up, fetched another rope, tied the two legs of the cow together and started milking.

'Make it fast,' called out his wife, 'otherwise you will not get your share of coffee.'

The sub-tenant silently pulled the teats until the black container was full to the brim with warm white foam. He handed the milk to Namaga's wife and untied the calf so that it would suck its mother's udder dry.

When the coffee was over the three couples left;

the men to get ready to go to the Afersata, and the women to their daily chores. Namaga, who was up till then in his nightwear, a huge cotton garment that required two men to wash it, got up from his mat to change his clothes. His daytime outfit consisted of a long shirt that reached the knees of his trousers, and a light veil-like shemma that he especially liked because it was all home-made. That morning he also wore his cork-hat and carried a white fly switch in his right hand.

The inhabitants of the thirty villages of Wudma arrived at the oak tree one by one. Some of them walked while others came on mule back. The governor of the sub-district of Wudma was present. So was the Cheka Shum. Everyone covered his head either with his hat or with his toga as there were hundreds of shrieking yellow birds overhead, which were occasionally letting fall their black and white droppings.

The governor explained the purpose of the gathering and told the villagers to elect seven elders to conduct the Afersata ceremony. Seven people were instantly nominated and the governor addressed the crowd by asking them: 'Do you all agree that the seven elders conduct the ceremony?' The crowd answered back with a shout of, 'We agree. We agree. We agree.'

During the ceremony absolute secrecy was required. Each villager was questioned by the elders, and none except the elders were supposed to hear the words of the informer 'wof'. Thus, the questioning took place out of earshot, a few hundred yards away from the crowd. The spot for hearing witnesses was fixed and two villagers were sent away to dig a hole in the ground and to make a fire. One person was sent away to fetch a leafy branch of a tree called 'huretta' with which to conduct the ceremony.

In the meantime the seven elders got ready to take a solemn oath so that they would conduct the ceremony properly. Each elder stood before the crowd and took the following oath.

'If I reveal the name of the informer who saw or heard about the criminal,
If I don't expose the criminal indicated by the informer,
If I hide the truth about the crime,
Then, may God deprive me of all my offspring, and make me rootless.'

The seven elders then went to the fire, leaving the crowd behind. One of the village headman called each person by name and sent him to the elders to be questioned. As he was calling names the Cheka Shum took notes of those who were absent. In fact many villagers failed to come that day for some reason or another. Some were reported sick. Others were absent because it was their turn to keep the village cattle, or they were away from the villages. Of all the absentees the one that disturbed the Cheka Shum most was a fellow called Beshir. Beshir lived in Namaga's village and formerly had a dispute with him over a plot of land. Besides, his neighbours suspected him of having his hands in any underhand business that brought him a few cents.

The night Namaga's hut burnt down Beshir was not in the village. Two days earlier he was reported to have gone to Addis Ababa to see his uncle on his mother's side, and to beg him to pay this year's tax for him.

Beshir never had enough money to pay the tithe or the land rent or the tribute to his landlord. He had to beg his relatives to pay for him. If they refused to do so he would threaten to kill their goats. He had, indeed, killed goats that belonged to his close relatives at least twice before, and nothing had happened to him. They could not sue him in court because he was their kin; they could not ask him to pay them back because he sold almost all the cows he inherited from his father and owned no other property.

The Cheka Shum took note of him and listened to the headman calling names. One person from Namaga's village went to the elders to be questioned.

'Haven't you burnt the hut of Namaga?' asked the elders.

'No I haven't,' answered the fellow.

'Haven't you seen the person who burnt Namaga's hut?'

'No, I haven't.'

'Haven't you heard of the man who burnt Namaga's hut?'

'No, I haven't.'

'Then hold this leafy branch of the huretta tree and extinguish this fire saying, "If I do not tell the truth, may my offspring be exterminated from the face of the earth like this fire."'

The fellow extinguished the fire uttering the foregoing words.

'Sweep away the ashes of the fire saying, "If I did not tell the truth may my offspring be swept away like these ashes,"' said the elders.

The fellow did what he was ordered to do, and went back to the oak tree to join the crowd. The elders kept on questioning every individual who came to the Afersata.

By late afternoon it got windy. The dry leaves of the oak tree started to fall. The sun was getting pale and cold. The seven elders were tired of conducting the ceremony. The villagers were tired of sitting and talking. They were also anxious to go back home and mow grass for their cows, split wood for the evening fire and then rest. The Cheka Shum who was discussing this year's assessment of tax with the sub-district governor interrupted the discussion to suggest that the Afersata be postponed. 'The investigation cannot be finished today,' he said, 'and as there are many absentees we had better postpone the Afersata for some other time.'

The governor pulled out a heavy pocket watch from his trouser pocket and read 5 p.m. 'You are right! We must disperse the crowd as some people have to walk a long way,' he said.

The Afersata was postponed till mid-July. The governor's male servant brought the saddled mule, and held the strap of one stirrup tightly so that the saddle would not slip down as the heavy master mounted from the other side. The mule started to trot forward while the servant, a gun on his shoulder and a cartridge belt full of sparkling bullets around his waist, trotted behind.

The Cheka Shum, too, mounted his grey mule, and left the crowd. In a few minutes the oak tree was deserted.

A few days later a group of villagers were busy constructing a new hut for Namaga. The cylindrical wall was already finished, and they were now busy with the conical roof. The unthatched structure resembled something like a giant, half-open umbrella. The central pillar and the poles that fanned out from the central pillar to sustain the cobwebbed roof were like the handle, the ribs, and the screen of an umbrella.

Some of the villagers worked on the ground sharpening the ends of poles and smoothing their surfaces, while others stood on the scaffold to insert more of the poles into the framework of the roof and to tie them with ropes.

Namaga killed a young zebu that day, as was the custom. His fellow villagers rendered him their labour and services free of charge, and he owed them a lunch feast in return.

In view of the importance of the occasion Namaga did not forget to invite the Cheka Shum. His presence was always welcome on feast days.

On his arrival, just before lunch, the Cheka Shum looked at the new hut from various angles and commented on its apparent defects. 'The wall is too high, and the roof too low,' he said.

The village architect who was paid ten dollars to supervise the work jumped up at the comment of the Cheka Shum and explained why it was so. 'I had a lengthy argument with Namaga,' said the architect, 'he wanted to have the wall low and the roof high up in the air like the old huts. But, sir, these days we have changed the style of our huts. All the huts I have supervised this year have high walls and low roofs. High roofs unnecessarily waste precious poles and grass for thatching them. Besides, huts with low walls and high roofs age too soon, because in the long run the heavy roof twists the wall and damages the whole construction. What I advise is to have a deep foundation so that at night thieves cannot succeed in entering the huts by digging under the beams, and to have high walls to sustain the roof easily.'

The Cheka Shum stayed silent for a while and then rubbing his smooth chin with his palm said, 'So that's why you broke the roof?'

'Yes, sir, that's why I broke the roof,' reiterated the architect.

The Cheka Shum entered the new hut and examining its inside asked the architect, 'How wide is it?'

The architect measured the radius of the hut starting from the central pillar. He used the length of his feet to measure it, and said, 'Sixteen.'

'I thought it was much smaller than that. Judging from its outside appearance I estimated it to be not wider than fourteen,' said the Cheka Shum.

'I measured it at least half a dozen times before, sir, and knew that it was sixteen. I measured it again just now because otherwise you wouldn't believe me.'

'Why does it look so small in appearance then?'

'Because, sir, I broke the roof.'

Two young men entered the new hut each carrying a bundle of the enseta leaves. They untied the bundles and started to spread the green leaves on the floor of the new hut. Two other young men came in carrying huge baskets full of raw meat garnished with yellow fat. A small boy followed suit, a bunch of knives in his hands.

The Cheka Shum and the architect stepped out. 'I like the new style,' said the Cheka Shum.

'If you like it, sir, every villager will like it too.'

A child approached the workers with a kettle of water. 'Food is ready, wash your hands,' announced Namaga, and ran to the sub-tenant's hut to fetch a stool for the Cheka Shum. The child poured the water on the hands of the workers while they washed.

The Cheka Shum sat on the stool near the entrance of the hut while the villagers squatted on

C

the floor along the wall of the new hut. The wussa bread and raw meat were served to each person present. The Cheka Shum was given the knife with the ivory handle while the others used knives with horn handles. As there were not enough knives the young men cut the meat with the sharp edge of split bamboos.

'You should bless the criminal who set your hut on fire,' said the Cheka Shum jokingly, 'you have a much better one now.'

'I am pleased with the new one. But still I want the criminal to be caught,' said Namaga.

'The Afersata day is approaching fast; only a few weeks left,' said Argaw, and added, 'those who were absent last time have been fined fifty cents each.'

That was the normal fine for absenteeism, a price that did not bother anyone much. What was worse was that when a person failed to go to the Afersata he attracted people's attention. He could easily be suspected of having committed the crime for which the Afersata was held. 'Incidentally, is Beshir back from Addis Ababa?' asked the Cheka Shum.

'No one saw him in our village,' answered Namaga.

'He is always one of those who are the last to pay tax,' commented the Cheka Shum.

When the lunch feast was over Argaw left for home while the villagers resumed work.

'Did you hear what he said? Did you hear well

what the Cheka Shum said?' asked Mela, Namaga's friend who was working on the ground beside him.

'What did he say?' asked Namaga.

'Didn't you hear him say that Beshir is always one of the last to pay tax?'

'Is that news for you?'

'It is no news for me. What he said is true. Beshir never pays tax on time. That's why yesterday the agent of the landlord took away the only cow in his house, and both his wife and his child were weeping.'

'You mean the agent took away the red cow as surety?'

'Yes, yes. That's what he did. And his wife was weeping because her child was weeping for lack of milk. I was very sorry for his wife and his child but not for him,' said Mela.

'Why not for him?'

'Because he is a bad guy. He never tills his plot and he never gets enough money to pay tax to the government or tribute to his landlord. I tell you his father was not like him. His father, Abza, (may his soul rest in peace) his father was a great man. He had one hut full of cows and zebus. At the time he died he had almost twenty head of cattle. But where are they now, all those animals, except the red cow that the landlord's agent took away as surety? I tell you they have all turned into water. Beshir sold them all and with the money he received he bought liquor instead. He drank with the money and the liquor passed through his body. I say he is a bad guy. He is so bad that after selling all the cows and zebus he started stealing the goats of his folks. I will not be a witness, but from what I hear he even steals clothes and guns and other things at night. Why, have you not seen him, walking with his face partly veiled with his toga?'

'Why so?'

'Because he does not want to be recognized by anyone,' said Mela, and wiping the saliva at the corners of his mouth with his palm added, 'you know what?'

'What?'

'I suspect. . . .'

'You suspect what?'

'May God forgive me if I am wrong. . . . I suspect he is the one who set your hut alight.'

The land-owning farmers of the thirty villages of Wudma paid only land tax and tithe to the government treasury. Others like Beshir and Namaga himself who cultivated the land of others had to pay in addition to the tithe and the land tax, a special tribute, *irbo*, to their absentee landlord. The amount of the *irbo* was entirely fixed by the landlord himself. Accordingly it varied from year to year depending on the harvest results and on the whim of the absentee landlord.

The tenants had no written contract with their landlords. They did not even have a formal oral contract. The present tenants as well as their ancestors had lived in the villages generation after generation for the past hundred years or so. So the land was sold and resold at various times without the knowledge of the tenants and they were even ignorant of their real landlords. They knew only the agents who lived there and collected the annual *irbo*.

If the *irbo* was too high an amount for the tenants to pay them, they could give up their plots and go away to some other place after being paid compensation for their crops. But as the standing crops like *enseta*, eucalyptus trees and coffee plants were estimated to cost more than the plot of land itself the absentee landlord would never chase away a tenant at the risk of paying him compensation. Instead, he exacted as much as he could short of chasing away the tenant.

'If I only had a piece of land of my own!' said Beshir in Addis, looking at his uncle with begging eyes, 'If I only had the slightest piece of land of my own, I would start working hard on it.'

'That is no excuse for shunning work,' reprimanded his uncle.

'But I don't want to sweat in order to fatten another man's pocket. If I work hard and earn more money my landlord would charge me more *irbo*. That's why I don't want to work hard,' he said.

'Whether you decide to work hard or not this is the last time that I shall pay tax of any kind for you. I have no money to waste on lazy people.'

Beshir's uncle received quite a few visitors from the countryside. His relatives came to see him in Addis for various reasons. Last year his cousin came to ask him for money to buy a mule. His niece came because she wanted to buy a dress. His folks in the country had inexhaustible reasons for coming to see him.

Although he was generous enough to give away money to the really needy relatives of his, he was fed up with those who begged simply because they did not want to use their hands.

Beshir's uncle was a government employee in one of the ministries. Although an insignificant civil servant by universal standards he was a big man in the eyes of his folks. It was even considered a miracle by them that one relative among them could be educated and be employed as a civil servant. In fact his 'success in life' had been the greatest impetus for his village folks to send their children to school.

Beshir's uncle fully understood the problems of his kind. His own father, before he died was a tenant like all the others. He even remembered an incident that took place in his father's hut when he was a child. The agent of his father's landlord came to collect the tribute which his father did not have ready at hand. The angry agent ordered his servant to take away the moveable door of the hut so that the father of the present civil servant would spend all night awake guarding his family and his property from thieves and wild animals.

Beshir's uncle was only a child at that time and couldn't even understand what was going on. But the memory of it was still fresh in his mind up to the present day.

Although the civil servant was fully aware of the problems of his folk he could not solve them to any appreciable extent. He was not important enough in the government to exert pressure to change the landholding system of the country. Only when his tenant folk came to see him he did whatever he could as an individual.

'Melesse could have become a rich man by now if his folk did not bother him now and then,' said his friends in Addis. That was true, but he did not have the guts to send away his relatives empty-handed. He was complying with the proverb that one cannot fill his belly and sleep with ease while his brother's stomach is empty. Melesse's policy was 'let's share whatever we have, and live happily'. But his folk sometimes went too far. They did not fully understand that he had to spend money on house rent, on food and all other expensive things purchased in Addis stores. They thought that he lived in his own house, that he spent only a dollar or two a day on food and drinks, and that he saved eighty per cent of his monthly salary of four hundred dollars. That's why they never believed him, when he told them that he had no money left in his pocket towards the end of the month.

'When are you going to see me off uncle?' said Beshir.

'You can leave tomorrow, at dawn,' said his uncle handing him out three notes of ten dollars each.

Beshir's face was all smiles. Since his plot was small and the crop on it rather meagre his share of tax and *irbo* was not much. He got more than he expected from his uncle, and the next morning he left for his village by bus.

On coming back home Beshir found his tiny daughter crying. 'What is wrong with the child?' he asked his wife.

'She is crying for lack of milk. Since the day the agent took away the red cow she has had nothing to drink but "black" water.'

'So he did take away the cow as he threatened to do!' he exclaimed, biting his lower lip with anger.

'He drove it away the day after you left for Addis.'

'I shall tell him who I am and who is my uncle!'

Beshir did not rest for more than half an hour before he left for the home of the agent, a small man with a round face. The agent had his hair cut unlike other villagers who had theirs clean shaven, and who believed that it was womanish to have one's hair cut and to have it combed every morning. Although the agent was illiterate like the rest of the villagers he tried to resemble city dwellers in various ways. In his youth he had lived in the capital as a pedlar selling needles, soap, combs, shoe laces and other petty articles. He spoke Amharic, the national language, without accent, a fact that made him feel superior to the villagers. The landlord selected him, among other villagers, to be his agent for the additional reason that he knew the streets of Addis in and out and that he could easily trace his way to the landlord's villa to present the annual tribute collected from the tenants.

'Where is my cow?' asked Beshir on his arrival, breathless and sweating.

'Where is the tribute?' asked the small agent in response.

'Where is my cow that you have stolen away in my absence?'

'I could have you imprisoned for what you have just said. I did not steal your cow, I just took it away as surety.'

'Perhaps you don't know me well enough. Otherwise you wouldn't dare take away the animal!'

'You are Beshir, if I am not mistaken, you who killed the goats of . . . I don't remember the name.'

Beshir got furious at the insulting words of the agent and held his cane up threateningly. 'I could kill you with one blow, you seller of needles,' he said, his voice trembling.

'I am the agent of your landlord. Don't forget that.'

'My uncle is as big a man as the master you serve.

He is a government official for your information.'

'I know that, you may spare your breath. But if I have you shackled at the sub-district court your uncle will not come to have you released. Remember that.'

'I am not afraid of your threats, you seller of needles, and I want my cow now.'

'Pay your tribute first, you killer of goats.'

There would have been a showdown if the Cheka Shum had not arrived by chance, at that moment. He was touring around the villages to order the headmen to press the farmers to pay the land tax and tithe as soon as possible. If the Cheka Shum failed to collect the taxes by the end of the fiscal year he would have to pay it from his own pocket or face imprisonment for failure to carry out his duty.

'What's wrong with you two? I could hear you arguing a mile off,' said the Cheka Shum.

'This fellow came to insult me instead of paying his tribute.'

'You are a liar. I came to pay you and to take back my cow that you had stolen in my absence.'

'Now cool down,' said the Cheka Shum, looking at Beshir, 'you should respect your superiors. Incidentally, you were absent last time we had the Afersata. You were informed about it, but you went away without any excuse.'

'I went to Addis Ababa to fetch money to pay tax, sir.'

'That isn't a sufficient excuse, and tomorrow

morning I expect you to bring to my house your share of tax and the fifty cents fine for absentee-ism.'

'Yes, sir.'

'And since it appears that you brought along with you money to pay the landlord's tribute pay it now instead of quarrelling.'

'Yes, sir, but I want my cow.'

'There is your cow,' said the agent pointing towards the half-starved animal that was tethered to a post.

Beshir threw the money in the agent's face in disgust and drove away the cow in the direction of his home.

Aga, the sub-tenant, came home wet to the marrow. Today it was his turn to tend the village cattle in the vast meadow in the middle of which stood the huge oak tree. His wife had told him, before he drove away his cattle, to carry the umbrella made of palm leaves as she guessed it would rain. He did, but the old umbrella with holes couldn't protect his huge body from the rain. Water was dripping from his shemma and from his loose shorts as he walked into the hut, following the cattle. Since he had no clothes to change into he sat down on a mat by the fire side to dry his drenched shemma and shorts. His night garment was the relatively heavy shemma that his wife wore during the day. 'Put more faggots on the fire woman, I am shivering,' he said.

'Let me first scrape away the dung from the entrance of the hut,' she said, 'what would people say if they dropped in by chance?'

'What people are you talking about? No-one will come at this hour of the evening.'

It was about seven o'clock. The sub-tenant certainly expected nobody at that hour. Namaga's new hut was already thatched, its floor was levelled, and it was occupied. If people came for the evening gathering they would enter the new hut and not that of the sub-tenant. The glory of the old hut was gone. Aga and his wife started their humble normal life with nobody calling at their place. But the sub-tenant's wife had not yet readapted herself to her old life that had been interrupted for some time during Namaga's occupation of the old hut. She was still worried that respectable people would arrive at any time in the evening.

When she finished scraping the dung and the mud carried into the hut on the hoofs of cows and zebus she straightened her back and looked round towards her husband. 'I thought the mud was brought in by the cattle only. But now I see!' she remarked sarcastically.

The sub-tenant was a little ashamed. His wife had told him several times, since the start of the rainy season, that he should clean his feet before entering the hut, an instruction he never remembered. He ran out of the hut and cleaned his feet by passing his spread out toes through the blades of grass. It was still drizzling outside.

'I hate the rain,' he said upon re-entering the hut.

'Really?' she said in a mocking tone.

'Yes, I hate the rain,' he said again seriously.

'You'd better not, man. You will get nothing to eat if no rain falls. The corn and pumpkin you have planted will not grow without rain.'

'Just the same I hate the rain. As you told me yourself one day I am like a goat when it rains.'

The sub-tenant's wife laughed aloud, and put more wood on the fire. She decided also to bring him dinner earlier than usual so that they would sleep together soon and feel warm. During the day both were so occupied with routine work that they forgot themselves completely. It was only at night that they felt they were living. Only when they breathed on each other's face, and touched each other's body, only then were they conscious of their being in the world.

'Haven't you brought any wild mushrooms from the meadow?' she asked.

'The village children collected them all before I drove my cattle to the meadow.'

'Too bad. You will have only cooked cabbage to eat your wussa-bread with,' she said.

'Bring the food. I am hungry.'

She brought the cooked cabbage in a large clay bowl and wussa-bread in a flat clay dish.

'The village headman was here this afternoon,' she said as they were eating dinner.

'Whatever for?'

'He said the Afersata will take place two weeks from today.'

'Did he have to announce it so early, then?'

'I don't know anything about it. I am a woman and that's men's business. I have just told you what he asked me to tell you.'

'If all people worked there would be no thieves and criminals. And if there were no thieves there would be no Afersata.'

'I just said I don't know anything about these things. That is not women's business.'

'All right. Forget it,' he said.

When the meal was over the sub-tenant's wife stored away the black clay bowls while her husband washed his feet. After a short while she untied the sash from her waist and slept beside him near the fire-place.

The sub-tenant and his wife had no children. They did what they could and prayed that God would grant them at least one child. But he would not.

'If we had a son he would keep cattle for me,' the sub-tenant said.

'And if we had a daughter she would fetch water for me,' his wife answered.

As the fire consumed itself into ashes the inside of the hut got dark, and the sub-tenant and his wife interlaced into each other's arms.

'Beshir's son was in the meadow this morning,' he said after a while, 'and the red cow was also there.'

'Really?' she said in a careless tone.

'Yes, and the child told me that his father brought a large amount of money from the city. His uncle on his mother's side is a big man, they say, and he "eats" four hundred dollars in one month. And Beshir came back from the city with a large amount of money.'

'What's that to you?'

'I am just telling you. Don't you want to listen?'

'All right tell me more.'

'I have finished,' he said.

'You are a fool,' she said.

'Are you insulting me?'

'On the contrary, I am praising you,' she said and burst out laughing. 'Anyhow you haven't heard half of the story,' she continued. 'I met his wife in the market place this afternoon. She was wearing a new dress and buying fresh cheese. The market women who knew her came to admire her dress and to feel its quality by holding the stuff between their fingers. They said it was even better than the dress of the agent's wife. Of course those who did not know that Beshir had an uncle in the big city suspected that the dress was a stolen one. Others were so jealous of her that they did not want to say anything about her dress. They just saw it and went away.'

The sub-tenant scratched his itching back, and while doing so he partly uncovered his wife's legs, thus exposing them to the cold. 'Don't move,' she said, 'sleep quietly.'

'The fleas are biting me,' he said.

'Don't you move again. If your back needs scratching I will do it for you. But for God's sake don't make my legs bare.'

They kept on talking and arguing for sometime until they were overcome by sleep.

2 *Son of A Tenant*

Melesse, Beshir's uncle, had not visited his native village for the last five years. Since his father had died while he was in high school, and his mother, two years later there was nothing that could induce him to go back home.

His native place was rivers away from the thirty villages of Wudma, and when Tekle, his friend and colleague, had asked him some time ago to take him there Melesse had told him that he couldn't go there because his father's plot was long abandoned.

Tekle was from one of the northern provinces. The idea of visiting the Gurage land had been with him ever since he was a student of social science at the university college of Addis Ababa. But so far his wish had not been fulfilled. Once he even decided to take the bus and travel as a tourist all by himself. But another friend of his convinced him that it would be a waste of time and energy to go there without a proper guide. It was only then that Tekle changed his mind, and instead decided to look out for someone who could show him the Gurage land in and out. But the only person he could find was his bosom friend Melesse.

One Sunday morning as the two were taking coffee with milk in a bar, Tekle brought the matter shrewdly to Melesse's attention. 'Why don't we go out of this town and see some new places, Melesse? The weather is disgusting here. It is raining day in and day out. Let's go somewhere for a change.'

'Where to? Isn't it raining everywhere in Ethiopia at this time of the year?'

'Let's go to the country until the end of our annual leave. We still have five days more to go and life will be boring staying here all that time doing nothing.'

'But this is the worst season of the year to go to the country. In Addis at least we have the privilege of walking on asphalt streets while the country is only a stretch of half solid earth. The rivers are high and dirty, and in general life is worse there than it is here.'

'You promised me one day to show me your native village, and now is the time for it.'

'Did I?'

'Of course you did.'

'I don't remember having promised you anything of the sort,' said Melesse, 'but, anyhow I don't mind at all taking you to the south if you are ready to face the rain and the mud.'

'Don't bother about me. I was born in the country myself and know how to walk in the mud. As for the rain I am no salt to dissolve in it.'

They decided to leave the next day by the eight o'clock bus, and left the bar to prepare their suitcases, their boots and umbrellas.

Melesse and Tekle set off to the village of Beshir and not to the village Melesse was born. Melesse intentionally avoided his native village because first of all he thought that it would be difficult for them to find lodging there, and secondly since he had been told that his father's plot was covered with thorny bushes and weeds he was afraid that he would be filled with self-pity. He was also afraid that the mere sight of his native village would be a cause of nostalgia – of remembrances of things past and buried in his mind not to be recalled again. But alas, the mere sight of a village was sufficient to bring back everything he had forgotten, and to place it, so to speak, before him in broad daylight.

Melesse felt sad. He recalled his father who treated him like a pet, rubbing his hair, wiping his running nose with his bare hand, and teaching him how to touch his nose with the tip of his tongue. He once competed with his father in another game – passing the saliva between the teeth. His father's front teeth were set wide apart and he could throw out his saliva in a straight line after stretching out his lips, and tightly clenching his white teeth. Melesse tried hard to imitate his father but he could not because his front teeth were set close together.

Strangely enough Melesse recalled only the small things of his childhood days. He thus remembered an incident that caused his mother terror. That was the day he had difficulty in swallowing the wussa-bread. His mother who had only a few cents to buy cheese gave him a dry piece of bread to eat. The child chewed one bite and tried to swallow it. But the bread stuck in his throat so that he could neither throw it out or swallow it. His mother who saw him struggling with himself trying to breathe ran to fetch water. She came back with a cup half full of water and tried to make him drink it with the bread. But the boy, instead of swallowing the liquid, struggled to push down the bread in a vain effort. His mother thought he was dying, and gave him a terrible blow on the back that forced the bread down his throat. After the blow she began to weep frantically. 'I am all right mother. It was just a crumb that tried to pass through my wind-pipe,' he said. But she kept on weeping and sob-bing. 'You almost died my son. And simply because

I could not afford to buy you cheese,' she said.

Melesse recalled various other things – his child-hood friends, the trees they used to climb like little devils, the games they used to play: swimming in the high dirt-laden river, slipping down the wet, muddy hillsides on their bare buttocks, running around in search of wild mushrooms, and so on, and so on.

Melesse and Tekle were splashing the muddy flood beneath their high boots when Tekle said, 'It is remarkable!'

'What is remarkable?' asked Melesse distractedly.

'The villages in this side of the country are quite different from those I expected to see. I always knew that the walls of the huts were not rectangular and that the roofs were a little different from ours in the north. But I never knew that the villages were so crowded with huts.'

'You should know the reason.'

'To tell you frankly I don't.'

'Well, it's rather simple. It's the type of cultivation that brings about the difference. In the northern provinces, and as a matter of fact everywhere in Ethiopia outside the enseta culture complex, people need a large expanse of land to grow cereals. In such places you see a cluster of four of five huts and you travel for miles before you see another cluster of huts. In this part of the country up to twenty families can live on a gasha, forty hectares, of land. An average number of fifty enseta plants are sufficient for a family of four, for a year. You don't need a large expanse of land for that purpose.

This does not of course mean that the farmers in this part of Ethiopia have as much land as they need for cultivation. On the contrary, many complain that their plots are too small.

As you know my folks are among those tribes of Ethiopia which migrate most. You find them practically in all towns and cities. They either go into commerce or live independently as crafts-men or offer their services and labour to individuals or organizations in the cities. The explanation for their migration is that they do not have a sufficient amount of land to cultivate. A father dies leaving, say, four children behind him. They divide his small piece of land among themselves and start cultivating it, only to pass a still smaller piece to each of their children. In that way the share of each child dwindles from generation to generation, the result being the migration of some of them to the towns and to the cities.'

'If a family can live on fifty enseta plants why is it then that I see hundreds of them behind each hut?' asked Tekle, 'Do they sell the rest?'

'Well, the ones that you see immediately behind the huts are still in the nursery stage. It takes about seven years for the young plants to reach maturity. There are at least four stages in the cultivation of the plant. First of all the roots must be buried in the ground in such a way that dozens of shoots sprout out from them. Then the shoots must be taken apart and planted separately. Then they must be transplanted each year for at least three years, which means that a man who wishes to process fifty ensetas into bread must own at least four hundred plants in the four stages of growth.'

'I see,' said Tekle, 'but do they actually sell the plant?'

'Of course, they do. A big enseta plant may sell for up to five dollars. Incidentally this shows you clearly why a landlord never wishes to chase away a tenant from his land. It is too costly for the land-lord to pay the tenant compensation.'

As they approached Beshir's hut the village children who were playing in the open field looked at them curiously. They knew they were from another world – their high boots, their rain coats, their closed umbrellas and their suit-cases attested that they were people of the city.

The arrival of Melesse at the village was a great surprise for Beshir. He had seen him in Addis only a few days ago and at that time Melesse did not even mention his coming. His surprise was mingled with pride. He knew what that meant in the eyes of the villagers, and especially in the eyes of the landlord's agent who had stated with conviction that Beshir's uncle would not come back to the country to have Beshir released if he had him shackled in the sub-district court. Melesse's arri-val boosted Beshir's morale and instilled in him

a new feeling of confidence he had never exper-
ienced before. Now that it was proved that Addis
was very close and that Melesse might come to the
village at any time no one would dare insult Beshir
or belittle him by calling him seller of goats or
something like that. As he proved to the thirty
villages of Wudma that he could receive and enter-
tain two 'important' government employees in his
hut his fellow villagers would realise his importance and take him more seriously from now on.
Beshir felt very elated.

Tekle examined the inside of Beshir's hut, the
floor mat made of jute by the co-operative work
of the village women; the fired clay wares that
decorated the walls in three horizontal rows;
wooden stools and wooden materials for washing
the feet and clothing; bamboo tables; umbrellas
made of palm leaves and a score of other locally
made objects that made him change his false
opinion about Melesse's folks. 'I am somewhat
ashamed of myself,' he said finally, looking at
Melesse.

'What do you find to make you feel ashamed of
yourself?'

'My ignorance.'

'About what?'

'About your folks and their way of life. I used to
think that the Gurage were simply porters in Addis,
shoe-shiners, and pedlars. Now I see a people with
a distinct culture and a respectable way of life.'

'You are not the only person who has a wrong

image of my folks. Half of the town dwellers have the same ideas as you had before. And besides you still don't know much about my folks. You have so far seen only the insignificant symbols of their culture.

Before the unification and centralization of Ethiopia in the nineteenth century the Gurage lived in a stateless society. Laws were made directly by the people themselves as in the old Greek city states. The chiefs and the elders certainly played the most important role in this matter, but the assembly under a tree was open to anyone who wished to be present and give his opinion about any matter concerning society as a whole. There was no established army to defend that stateless society, but every male adult was a soldier in time of outside threat. There was no police force to ensure peace, but society as a whole was responsible for any crime committed by an individual. Thus, if a person murdered another, either he would be exiled from his motherland or his tribe would contribute money for him to pay the blood price. This type of collective responsibility is still practised among the Gurage today as it is practised elsewhere in Ethiopia. The institution of Afersata, for instance, is based on the philosophy of collective responsibility.'

'That is true, but I wouldn't call the Afersata a good national institution. The farmers suffer because of its existence,' said Tekle.

'What alternative is there to it?'

'There should be a police force to investigate crimes.'

'That's easy to say brother. But there can be a police force only if there is money to establish and maintain it. But where can that money come from except from the farmers themselves who already have to pay land tax, tithe, *irbo*, education tax, health tax, etc.?'

'Payment of tax exists everywhere in the world. It is a national obligation.'

'I agree with you on that point, but how can you call payment of *irbo* a national obligation? It is in fact a national vice. I understand that in the northern provinces every farmer is his own landlord. But here it is not like that.

When people lived in a stateless society there were no landlords and tenants. Everybody cultivated his own or the community land. Less than a century ago, however, a few people mysteriously became landlords and the others *irbo* payers in this part of the country.'

Beshir's wife was melting butter while Melesse and Tekle were arguing about the land tenure system of the country. Vapour from the boiling butter entered their nostrils. There was also a strong smell of spices that made the Addis Ababans sneeze now and again. 'The peasants are getting poorer while the absentee landlords are getting richer,' stated Melesse after a while, 'if the government does not distribute land to the peasants they will never be better off in the future.'

'But a land reform ministry has been established not so long ago.'

'I wonder what that ministry is going to do. You think it is going to dispossess the landlords and distribute their lands to the peasants?'

'I don't think that is the intention. And even if that were the intention on my part I wouldn't consider it just to dispossess those who acquired their land by genuine labour and purchase.'

'By genuine labour!' exclaimed Melesse laughing with contempt for the landlords, 'Most of the land that belongs to the absentee landlords in this country is either an outright grant made by the government or property acquired by paying a nominal price for it. Only a minor part was bought and sold by individuals.'

'Even if it is a grant nobody should be dispossessed of his property.'

'Well, Ethiopia belongs to every Ethiopian. In time of war the peasants are expected to take up their arms just like the absentee landlords. In time of peace they give part of their produce to the government by way of tax, just like the absentee landlords. Therefore they must be entitled to some land of their own. In fact this country will never become rich without a proper land reform.'

'The country's future does not entirely depend on land reform. What we actually need is industry. Look, for instance, at the miracle done by the Wonji Sugar Factory. In a matter of fifteen years this factory is capable of producing enough sugar for home consumption, and even of exporting some to other countries. The amount of tax collected from that company is not negligible either. I heard that the company paid over ten million dollars this year alone to the government treasury.'

'I never said industry is not needed for this country. But your statement that the Wonji factory supplies a sufficient amount of sugar for the whole empire and even exports some bags needs qualification. Do you know, for instance, the per capita consumption of sugar in Ethiopia at the present time?'

'No, I don't.'

'It is less than three kilograms a year, which means the lowest rate in Africa. And my next question is why is it so low?'

'I don't know exactly, although I believe there is no demand for it.'

'That is right, but why is there no demand for it?'

'Simply because people are not interested in it.'

'There you are mistaken, brother. It is not because people are not interested in sugar, but because they cannot afford the luxury of it. So instead of sugar they use salt which is cheaper. This means, that your Wonji factory exports sugar not because it prefers to but because it cannot sell it in the home market for the price it demands. This shows you clearly that the mere establishment of factories does not make the people better off. Factories must have an extensive market where they can sell their products. Otherwise it would not be much use having them.'

'Do you mean then that land reform is going to solve this problem?'

'Yes, indeed, at least partly. Land reform, that is the distribution of land to the peasants will stimulate them to work. That is in fact what my cousin Beshir told me a few weeks ago when he came to see me in Addis. He told me he does not want to work hard because his landlord charges him as well as all the other tenants whatever tribute he wishes to charge. Besides, even if the amount of the tribute were fixed, as is done in some cases, the tenant still wouldn't work as hard as he could otherwise.'

'I still don't see the connexion between land reform and the sale of sugar.'

'Don't be so pretentious. Land reform means more work for the peasants. More work means more production of agricultural goods. That in turn means more money for the farmers. And finally if they have money they can buy sugar. Thus land reform must start with the redistribution of land among those who need it.'

'I still don't agree with you on this point. What reasons have you got to dispossess the landlords?'

'You didn't listen to me, it appears. But I told you the reason before. The land always belonged to the people who cultivated it. Their fathers and their grandfathers owned that land. For less than a century their lands have been mysteriously transferred to the absentee landlords. Now the land must be given back to the peasants.'

'You are infected by foreign ideas, it seems to me. There have always been poor people and rich people throughout the history of man. If there are landowners and peasants in Ethiopia it is not something unheard of, and one should not be sentimental about it.'

'There has always been disease too, in the history of man. But on that account people have not been indifferent to those diseases. They discovered medicines and abolished at least some of them. Your indifference is similar to saying that there has always been malaria in Ethiopia; why should anyone be sentimental about it?'

'Your comparison is unrealistic.'

'It couldn't be more realistic. For what is indeed the relation between the indolent landlord and the tenant farmer except that of a mosquito and its victim?'

'But the whole idea is foreign to Ethiopia.'

'What you should consider in this case is not the source of the idea. What you must ask yourself is whether the idea is right or wrong and not whether it comes from the moon or from the centre of the earth.'

'But the landlords have a right to their property. Don't forget that.'

'I am not talking of those who have genuinely bought their land and who cultivate it, brother. I am talking of those who got it for nothing, and who do not make any use of it.'

'What do you mean by that?'

'I mean those who got it by *dedje tenat*. In former times an important person would be granted hundreds of hectares of land simply because he was important and he asked for it repeatedly. Since such land was granted as a favour the owner cannot talk of his right to that land, because he never had a right to it. Or take another instance. Again an important person might have been given thousands of hectares of land so that his dependants, that is, the farmers, would cultivate it and pay him some tribute as a sort of salary for his administrative function. In the long run the fellow would claim that the land was his personal property while in actual fact it never belonged to him. In my opinion the land acquired in this manner should be redistributed to the peasants who cultivated it. Otherwise land reform in Ethiopia will exist only on paper.'

'You are going too far in this matter Melesse. Dispossessing the landowners will bring about strife and social unrest.'

'There will be worse strife if land reform does not become a reality, I mean when the people become conscious of their situation.'

'Anyway this is a government affair, I don't want to interfere in something that is outside my domain,' said Tekle wishing to drop the discussion.

'This is not outside your domain. You are a citizen of this country and you have the right to express your opinion on such matters. Freedom of speech is guaranteed by the constitution and you have not only a right but a social obligation to express yourself.'

'In that case I should tell you that you are arguing from a theoretical point of view. I don't see the justice of dispossessing some in order to enrich others. The emphasis should be on supplying land to those who have none, which is actually being done, without impoverishing those who already have it.'

'Do you mean to say that a peasant should be driven out of the land in which his ancestors have been buried and on which he poured his sweat?'

'You are again becoming sentimental about the peasant's situation. What they want is land. Therefore they should be willing to go and work elsewhere, outside their own village.'

'You are arguing from an impractical point of view, Tekle. A man, say, who was born in this village and who lived here for thirty years would never be willing to go and reclaim virgin land a thousand miles away from his native village. He would rather stay here and lead a wretched life than go away and become prosperous. You know how much attachment there is to one's fatherland among our uneducated folks. And besides the land they cultivate is in reality theirs and not the property of the absentee landlord. Therefore the type of distribution you are talking about simply cannot be executed.'

'And according to you the only possible solution is to dispossess the landlords and give away their lands to their tenants?'

'That is the solution, although I admit that if an absentee landlord wishes to cultivate a piece of land he should be allowed to do so like everyone else. The rest of his land must be given to those who are actually farming it.'

At this point, Beshir who had gone away to fetch local beer came back with four bottles. 'I am somewhat surprised, although I confess I am happy about it, that you came to our village,' he said putting down the bottles on the floor.

'Why so?' said Melesse, turning his attention towards him.

'Because there is nothing that pleases a man here. In Addis you have everything: good drinks, good food, good clothing and clean rooms. You have for instance, a separate room for talking, another one for sleeping, another one for cooking, and another one for relieving yourself. Here we have one room for all purposes, and even then it is not as clean as your lavatory. Our lot here is to toil but not to live comfortably.

'We toil too,' said Melesse.

'Ha ha!' Beshir chuckled, 'What you call toiling is sitting down comfortably on a smooth chair and smearing black ink on a piece of white paper. I wish I were toiling too, like you I mean.' He laughed loudly.

'It's not really as easy as you think. Mental work can be very tiring.'

'You try to deceive me because I don't know how to read and write. But as far as I know our school children are toiling as much as you do – they, too, scribble something in their exercise books every day.'

'It's not the scribbling that is so tiring,' intervened Tekle, 'thinking is tiring.'

'Who does not think? We think more than you do. We think of how to get money in order to pay the *irbo*, of what to kill for the Maskel Festival, or where to get clothing for our wives and children. We think and worry continuously.'

There was no way of convincing Beshir that administrative and intellectual work could be tiring. As far as he was concerned the work of government employees was no more serious than an interesting hobby. 'Don't forget to roast the minced meat on the iron griddle,' he reminded his wife, 'people of the city are afraid of eating anything raw.'

'I won't forget,' she said and went on preparing the kitfo, the most delicious food of the Gurage, consisting of minced meat mixed with a lot of liquid butter and spices.

Beshir's wife was an excellent housewife. Despite the fact that Beshir's skinny cow gave only a tiny cup of milk, Beshir was never ill-fed. His wife went to the open market place twice a week and always managed to buy him cheese or meat. And when important guests dropped in occasionally she never failed to prepare the kitfo.

Her quality was not limited to being an excellent housewife. In addition she was fertile and gave birth to children. As the reader will appreciate, being fertile was among the top qualities of Gurage women. A husband could divorce his wife simply because she was naturally sterile. Love and beauty were values that were considered secondary to fecundity.

Why a child, and especially a son, has always been so desired and loved is a mystery; though there is a belief among the Gurage that a man who has children never dies, so to speak, but lives in his issue. A dead man is one who has no offspring. In fact when a person dies the first question asked about him is, 'Does he have children?' If the answer is positive then it is a great relief. If not, a sigh is followed by, 'Then he is blind!' meaning he has turned away from light forever, that he is totally annihilated from the face of the earth, and that he has become nothing.

When elders bless a person they say most often, 'May God give you a child,' or, 'May your child grow to be somebody.' If on the other hand they want to curse him, they say, 'May God never give you a child!' or, 'May you lose your children and thereby suffer!' A serious oath, as we have seen, has also something to do with a child. A child is thus a sort of possession of eternal life, and a fertile woman, the source of that eternity.

As country people have no pension their children, especially sons, are the only social security they have for old age and in time of sickness. The son has to take care of his parents' clothing, food and lodging when the mother and father are too old to work. It is also his obligation to take care of the burial expenses and the subsequent feast for the dead, the *tezkar* which takes place a couple of months after the date of the burial ceremony. Even at an earlier age a child is indispensable to his parents, for otherwise who will run errands, who will fetch water from the river, who will gather faggots for the fireplace, and who will tend the young calves? A man or a woman who is childless is called *metayo*, that is, one who has no helper, and such a person is very much pitied.

In Gurage village life a man who has many sons is respected and feared even if he is poor, for his children are his defendants on any occasion. For all these reasons the Gurage crave for children, and for as many of them as possible.

Nevertheless polygamy is rare in Gurage society. It would indeed be very difficult to meet a man who has three or more wives at the same time. Bigamy (having two wives simultaneously), however, exists, although not on an extensive scale. Bigamy is prac- tised among traditionalists, Moslems, and even Coptic Christians. It is non-existent among the Catholics, and the Protestant who has no roots in Gurage land.

Gurage husbands who practise bigamy settle their wives fairly far apart from one another. The rivalry between the wives is usually very tense. If they live too close to each other they may resort to fist fighting and hair plucking. If they are far enough from each other severe competition arises in pleasing the husband, each woman trying to keep him to herself for as long as possible. The husband stays longer with the wife he prefers although on certain important occasions like the Maskel festival he first celebrates the feast with the senior wife and then goes to the junior wife. Bigamy is an excellent institution for a husband who can afford to maintain two wives. But its effect may be disastrous for the children. For instance, if one of the wives dies her children will be obliged to live with the bitter foe of their mother. The surviving wife hates the mere sight of her rival's children and usually maltreats them. The husband may protest, but he cannot stay at home all the time to watch what is happening. The surviving wife will reduce such orphans to the status of servants, loading all the burden of the house on their tender shoulders.

Beshir's wife had no rival for the obvious reason that Beshir could not afford that luxury. Besides, as she had all the qualities expected of a Gurage wife, the fear of one day having a rival did not even cross her mind.

Beshir's wife finished preparing the kitfo and brought it before her honourable guests from the big city. Tekle, after throwing a glance at the minced meat totally drowned in the liquid butter, whispered to Melesse, 'I am afraid of the butter. It may be too heavy for my stomach.'

Tekle had previously tasted the kitfo in one of

the 'traditional' hotels of Addis. But what he tasted there was quite different from the kitfo that was placed before him. 'You have to try the real kitfo,' said Melesse, 'Addis hotels offer you only the imitation and not the genuine kitfo. First of all very often they mix butter with oil and present it as if it were pure butter. Secondly they are so stingy with it that you hardly feel the greasy part of the food.'

'Still I can't take it as it is,' said Tekle.

'Well, let me tell you an anecdote. After you hear it perhaps you will start drinking the liquid butter alone,' said Melesse laughing. 'When I was a child,' he continued, 'my mother used to give me, during the Maskel week, a cup of liquid butter every morning. She was giving it to me – perhaps you will not believe me when I tell you the truth, – she was giving me, as I was saying, a cup of liquid butter to sniff into my nostrils.'

'Whatever for?' asked Tekle.

'Everybody in the village, including my own poor mother, believed that sniffing liquid butter into the nostrils made a child handsome.'

Tekle laughed and commented at his friend's appearance by telling him that the liquid butter he sniffed into his nostrils did not really help much to improve his ugly but manly appearance.

'Be that as it may, brother, but take up your horn spoon and start eating,' said Melesse.

Beshir, who understood that Tekle was not willing to eat the kitfo as it was picked up Tekle's share and poured the liquid butter into a clay dish.

Then he ordered his wife to bring fresh cheese to mix with the minced meat.

'I know, you city dwellers do not like greasy substances, but we, without our butter, would not live long,' said Beshir, 'the inner surface of our stomach and intestine would crack open without grease,' he added, laughing at his own fantastic imagination.

Beshir's wife did not sit with the males for dinner. The guests begged her with all the courtesy of young city dwellers to sit down and eat with them, but she bashfully refused to do so.

'I have to feed my children now,' she said, 'I shall eat later on.'

The guests slept quietly and left for Addis the next day at about the same time that Beshir set off for the second Afersata.

3 *The Maskal Festival*

Namaga mostly blamed Beshir for the doubt in-
culcated in the mind of the villagers concerning
his loss of two hundred dollars. While it was obvious to everyone that a chicken and a few sacks of
coffee grains had been destroyed together with
Namaga's burnt-down hut there was no way of
finding out whether any money had been lost that
night. Consequently people strongly questioned
the validity of Namaga's claim.

If the villagers did not take Namaga for a tight-
fisted fellow, a lover of money, he would have told

them – without the slightest inhibition – where he had put his money, and how he had lost it, thereby clarifying the whole situation. But the villagers took him for a miser and he knew it.

On the morning of the second Afersata day Namaga decided not to reveal how he lost the money. He was ready to swear that he did lose it, but he would not reveal on any account, where the money was hidden at the time it was lost. 'How can I confess in public that I hid my money in the ground?' he said to himself, 'How can I say such a thing at the cost of confirming the villagers' false belief that I am a miser? Why, didn't Mela propose twice that I should buy a mule, and didn't I tell him twice that I couldn't afford it! What would he think about me now if I confessed that I buried all that sum in the ground? No! No! I shall never reveal where I hid my money. That's no one's business but mine!'

Namaga stored away that sum for cases of emergency. Only he and his wife knew about its existence. 'In case something happens,' he said to his wife the night they buried it in the ground near the central pillar, 'just in case I die or you die there will be cash at hand for the funeral expenses.'

The two hundred dollars were in hard currency; coins of twenty-five, ten, and five cents. Namaga was too careful to bury paper money. White ants could eat away the notes and cause a tragedy. Namaga dug a hole beside the central pillar, that night, while his wife put the coins in a clay jar the mouth of which she plugged with rags, covered it with large leather band and tied it tightly with a rope. Namaga buried it there, in the hole, and levelled the ground so that nobody would suspect its existence. The same night his wife covered the levelled ground with a mat.

'I still don't understand how this could happen. The night we hid away the money – mind you it was after midnight – at the moment we buried it there was no one around.'

'It is mysterious to me, too,' she said, looking rather sad, 'the thief must have come across it by sheer chance. Otherwise how could he calculate and dig from outside in order to find the very hole where the jar was placed? That would be impossible.'

'Nothing is impossible today woman, that is exactly what the thief did before setting my hut alight,' he said, and left for the second meeting of the Afersata.

People arrived by hundreds, and filled the compound of the sub-district governor. This time the Afersata was not held under the oak tree, for the grass was too wet to sit on, and the villagers were also afraid of the spirit of the sky that could strike the oak tree at any moment and cause damage to the crowd.

When the compound of the sub-district court was full the Cheka Shum, who was holding the roll book, called out names one after another, while his headman acted as a loud speaker.

'Beshir Safo!' shouted the headman, and ordered him to approach the elders.

'Have you burnt Namaga's hut?' asked the
elders.

'No, I haven't,' Beshir answered.

'Have you seen the man who burnt it?'

'No, I haven't. I was not even in the village that
night.'

'Have you heard of the man who burnt it?'

'No, I haven't.'

The elders made him swear using the huretta
tree. Various people who were absent during the
first Afersata were called to be questioned. This
time the number of absentees was reduced to
almost none.

The meeting was proceeding smoothly and
everyone hoped that this would be the last Afersata
on the burning of Namaga's hut. But unfortunately
the clouds in heaven gathered together into a thick
black mass, thunder struck on the surrounding hill
tops, and the sky split open with blinding flashes
of lightning; thus letting down a mixture of rain
and hail, and dispersing the crowd. The villagers
started to run like children who had heard their
teacher pronounce: 'break!' The governor, the
Cheka Shum, and a few elders hastened towards
the governor's residence, while all the others
rushed to the nearest shelter.

The rain came down in a torrent, and would
not stop for almost an hour and a half. On that
day many a hut leaked. It often happened that

vultures and other big birds perching on the thatched huts made holes in the roofs trying to catch
beetles and other insects that inhabited the straw.

'It is too bad we have to postpone the Afersata
once again,' said the governor, looking at the
round, white hail, the size of peas, outside the
governor's residence. A group of children, some
half-clad, others well wrapped up in their cotton
shemma, were playing in the rain, rolling the ice
balls into their mouths or throwing them at their
playmates. None of the children wore shoes. And
yet they did not feel the cold. The excitement was
too great for them to feel the dampness of the
earth. Some were in fact sweating despite the rain,
for they were running, chasing their playmates,
and flinging the ice balls at them.

'Until what date shall we postpone the Afersata?'
asked the Cheka Shum. 'As it would be useless to
convene the people during this dark season we
shall have to postpone it till the end of the Maskal
Festival. By then the earth will be dry and the sky
clear. That would also give the villagers ample
time to look for the criminal and witness against
him.'

It was agreed.

Two days before the Maskal Festival the blacksmith's workshop – a thatched roof standing on
four vertical poles – was crammed with people.
A few children were squatting on the ground
waiting impatiently for their turn to have their

knives sharpened, while others stood carrying their bundles on their shoulders. Adults who had no children had to come in person, in which case the village blacksmith did them the favour of sharpening their knives before those of the children.

Aga, the sub-tenant, arrived with a bundle of sickles, some of which were broken and others toothless from age and use. The children looked at him, and then at each other, and they laughed loudly with excitement as if they saw something funny for the first time in their lives. The black-smith noticed the tools in the hands of the sub-tenant and could not restrain himself from laughing as well.

On one side of the workshop, very close to where the blacksmith worked, there was a pile of coal from which the fire was fed. The metal parts of the knives were glowing in the fire. Their blades pointed towards the centre while their handles fanned out in a circle round the fire.

The blacksmith sat on a log, purposely naked above his waist. Sweat ran down his earth-brown cheeks. Beads of warm sweat dripped also from his short beard and landed on the ground. 'There is a smell like burnt horn, boy, watch out for the handles!' he said, addressing his apprentice. Then he drew a knife from the fire and holding it by its horn handle laid the red hot metal on the anvil. He raised his right hand above his massive shoulder and brought down the iron hammer heavily on the edge of the metal. He struck repeatedly on the metal, starting from the pointed end and working towards the broadest part of the blade, indenting the part on which the hammer fell. He turned the edge of the knife and struck again and again until the metal flattened out into a thin sheet at both edges.

He took another one from the fire and continued striking. His entire body shook as he struck blow after blow. His face contracted. He clenched his teeth. A vein on his forehead stretched out like an angry snake. His muscles jumped in his forearms like restless mice, and the sweat kept on dripping from the end of his short beard.

The villagers never addressed him as a blacksmith, a pejorative term that all blacksmiths frowned upon. They called him instead 'Ije Work', which means literally, 'hand-of-gold'.

'I brought my sickles, hand-of-gold,' said the sub-tenant. The children winked at each other mischievously and burst out laughing once again.

'I brought my sickles, hand-of-gold,' he said again, ignoring the children. 'Won't you do me the favour of sharpening them now?'

The blacksmith stopped striking for a moment, and after wiping his sweat with his bare arm he said, 'Don't you know that the Maskal Festival is in two days time, man? or perhaps you want to cut meat with sickles?' On hearing the words of the blacksmith the children laughed prolongedly all at once. 'He is a fool!' said a boy at last. 'He is stupid!' said another, and finally they shouted: 'He is a fool! He is stupid!' in chorus.

'Shut up boys! You should respect your elders,' snapped out the blacksmith, and turning his face towards the sub-tenant he added, 'what on earth made you think of bringing your sickles to-day?'

'I am going to start mowing the lawn in front of my hut. On Maskal day my cows must also feast,' said the sub-tenant.

'You don't need ten sickles for that purpose. Just one is sufficient, and if you want to do it yourself here you are,' said the blacksmith handing him a file, 'as for me I have no time for it. You see how many knives there are to be sharpened.'

'I hope I did not hurt your feelings, hand-of-gold,' said the sub-tenant, 'and if I did I swear to God I did not mean it.'

'You did not hurt my feelings. It's only that you lack common sense.'

The blacksmith resumed work while the sub-tenant started sharpening his sickle. The apprentice, a young boy of twelve and an orphan from the clan of the blacksmith, pressed the bellows to enliven the fire more. All the children wanted to press the bellows. It was a kind of game for them, but the apprentice stubbornly refused to let them do his work. 'Go away and play in the field until I finish sharpening your knives. And I don't want to see anyone of you disturbing my apprentice,' the blacksmith said, and added, addressing his apprentice, 'press it boy, press it hard and add more coal to the fire.'

The blacksmith received ten cents for every three knives he sharpened. It was during this season, every year, that he made his 'fortune'. He could not amass as much wealth even during the ploughing and planting seasons when every tenant came with a hand plough to be repaired.

Modern Christians associate the Maskal Festival with the finding of the true cross. The word Maskal literally means the cross. But the inhabitants of the thirty villages of Wudma, like many of their compatriots elsewhere in Ethiopia hardly attached any religious meaning to the Maskal Festival. It had existed since time immemorial, before the inhabitants themselves or their ancestors became Christians. It existed among the pagan Ethiopians and the only group of people that did not celebrate the Maskal were the Moslems.

The Maskal Festival falls in mid-September, the month that marks the end of the wet, rainy season, and the beginning of the bright, dry season.

In the mind of the villagers the rainy season is similar to the night. As the night is associated with fear, crime, insecurity and all the evil things in life, so is the rainy season. Snakes and vultures are supposed to be blind throughout that season. Life is hard, money and food are scarce. Travelling is difficult because of mud and rain.

September is the dawn of the bright sunny days. The Ethiopian New Year starts on the eleventh of that month, and the Maskal Festival sixteen days later.

'Are you going to kill a young zebu or something like that for the Festival?' asked the blacksmith.

'Me, kill a young zebu?' asked the sub-tenant with surprise.

'Why not? These days people who kill zebus are not much wealthier than you, like Beshir, for instance.'

'Is he going to kill a zebu?'

'Yes, indeed, although not a big one.'

'Well, he has a big uncle in the city. He was in the village a few days ago, and I suppose he gave him money once again.'

'And people say over a hundred zebus will be killed this year in the thirty villages of Wudma.'

'Good for you. You will collect plenty of meat. As for me I am going to buy meat for five dollars. That will be more than enough for my wife and myself.'

'Is the master (Namaga) going to kill a big one?'

'What do you think? He bought a huge one in a faraway market.'

The blacksmith had a vested interest in how many animals were butchered for the Festival and what size they were. The blacksmith, as well as the splitter of wood received from the person who killed a zebu a special organ of the animal, that is if the blacksmith and the woodworker did not charge any money for the services they rendered. The blacksmith usually collected part of the loin of the animal while the woodworker collected part of its neck.

[76]

'Good-day, hand-of-gold. I must go now,' said the sub-tenant rising from the ground.

'Good-day, man,' answered the blacksmith without turning his eyes from the edge of the knife he was flattening out.

The zebu that Namaga bought for the Festival was a ferocious one. It tried to run away from the stable three times, but three times it failed. It's hind leg was firmly tied to a pole in the sub-tenant's hut.

The day it was slaughtered Mela, Namaga's neighbour, tied another thick rope round its horns and holding the other end of the rope he went forward, while the sub-tenant pulled the animal from behind. Thus it was driven out of the hut between two men, one dragging it forward, the other pulling it backward in such a way that it would be impossible for it to run away. The two men with the help of some others felled it on the mown lawn just in front of Namaga's hut. The sub-tenant tied the two legs of the zebu together tightly, running the rope round and round the legs while Mela and a third fellow twisted the animal's neck and held it in such a way that its throat was turned towards the sky while its horns were planted in the ground. The fierce animal roared and tried to rise up and run away. But Namaga approached, a long sharp knife in hand, made the sign of the cross and bending down started to cut the throat with the steel knife. The zebu struggled to rise up once again, but in vain. Namaga slashed open a vessel and the blood splashed on his hand and clothes.

'Move away, all of you, move away. We are through with it,' said Namaga shouting.

'It will rise up if we let it go,' said Mela still holding its head down to the ground.'

'Move away, I say, it can't stand up.'

The sub-tenant, Mela, and the third fellow moved back. The animal groaned and struggled in a last effort to stand and flee. It managed to stand on its feet for a fraction of a second, but then it dropped heavily to the ground. It swayed its head in agony and smashed it to the ground again and again until its 'soul was out'.

'It's dead, let's skin it,' said Mela. Two others followed him, and after dragging the corpse away from the pool of blood they started skinning. Mela cut open the skin on its chest and looking at its flesh he commented, 'It's white like cotton. I wonder whether we shall be able to separate the skin from the fat.'

In a few minutes the skinning was over. The dismembering of the killed animal, however, was not an easy task to be executed by any layman. It required a real skill to cut out each organ according to long-established custom. Mela was an expert in this job, and so he was handed the sharpest knife to finish the work as soon as possible. Mela could have completed the task he was entrusted to in a matter of an hour if he had not been hampered by various things. First of all he had to chase away the dogs that smelt blood and came sniffing around to gnaw at bones. The vultures, too, that were supposed to be blind during the rainy season now hovered threateningly above his head. The village children, on the other hand, were standing around thus hindering Mela from freely moving his arms. At the end of about two hours everything was ready. Every organ was put in its proper place to be despatched. The lungs were cut up and distributed to the village children who were waiting impatiently for their *weret*, that is, their share. Part of the loin went to the village blacksmith, part of the neck to the wood-splitter. The hump was stored away in a basket before despatching it to Namaga's parents. If they had not been alive the hump would have been sent to Namaga's eldest brother. The freshly circumcised boys in the village got their share too, a special organ once again. And finally the village women who had given birth to children during the last two months (the period they stayed behind curtains) received their *weret*, the most tender part of the lean meat that is cut out of the animal's hind legs. All this was given away free of charge. That was Gurage custom.

Finally all the people who had helped fell the zebu and who took part in the skinning and dismembering of the poor animal gathered in Namaga's hut to eat their share in a group. Their share consisted of the stomach, the liver and the tongue, after casting away the tip of the tongue.

The Gurage believed that a man or a woman who eats the tip of an animal's tongue becomes talkative and restless. Therefore the tip was always cut away.

In principle the rest of the meat went to the family. The whole week following the Maskal day was consumed by members of his immediate family. The whole week following the Maskal day people of all walks of life came to wish Namaga and his family a happy new year, for the real new year for the Gurage started on the Maskal day. And every well-wisher was invited to eat, no matter at what time the person arrived. If the visitor was already full and resisted the invitation to a meat feast then Namaga would insist that there was always some vacant space in the stomach for more food, and the guest would finally agree, even if it were only to taste the meat. That was the Gurage way of life.

4 *The End of The Afersata*

At the end of September the countryside appeared at its best. The rain fell no more. The mud dried up and the black earth of Wudma started to crack with heat. The valleys and the hills were covered with blooming daffodils, and the sky was a spotless blue.

The peasants were happy after a full week of feasting and of rest. The cows and the zebus as well as the sheep and goats were well fed because of the abundant grass. September was the best time of the year for all living things.

But the Afersata was still to come. There was still fear in the heart of the bad men as well as in the heart of the innocent. Anyone could give wrong information at the expense of the person one disliked, and have him condemned for a crime he had never committed.

'Is there anything to eat, woman?' asked the sub-tenant addressing his wife, the morning of the Afersata day, 'I won't get anything to eat for the whole day under the oak tree.'

'I hope nobody will inform against you,' she said, dumping out into a wide container the green corn and the pumpkin she had just cooked, 'perhaps the master's hut burnt down by itself,' she added.

'How could that happen? Someone must have set it on fire.'

'You know that occasionally hot ashes scraped from the fire-place are dumped at the back of the hut. The wind could have blown the hot ashes into the straw of the roof, thus causing it to burn.'

'I don't believe it,' he said, and stretched his hand to the earthenware container to pick up a slice of pumpkin. 'Aw!' he cried and withdrew his hand, 'You are burning my fingers!'

'Good God gave you a pair of black eyes. Don't you see that I am dumping the food into the container?'

'That's no excuse for burning my fingers, woman.'

'You should be patient for a moment until I

present it to you in the proper way,' she reprimanded him, 'one would have thought that you had had nothing to eat for the last two days,' she added.

'Do you mean I am greedy, woman?'

'Act like a respectable man, at least in your own home. That's all I want you to do,' she said. Then fetching a bamboo table she put a few slices of the pumpkin, and some ears of the green corn on it and presented it to him.

Aga picked up one slice and peeled it off. 'It is of good quality,' he commented after biting off a piece.

'You could tell its quality by its look. It is red and solid.'

'That's right. But it's too hot!'

'Take your time. Let it cool off.'

'I have no time, woman. This is the last Afersata day.'

'It is too early to go to the Afersata. Even the master is at home.'

Namaga called out for the sub-tenant right at that moment to accompany him to the Afersata place. 'I told you, woman. Everybody is going early today.'

'Fill your belly before you go. I shall ask the master to wait for you for a moment,' she said and went out.

When the sub-tenant had finished eating he joined Namaga to go to the Afersata place. It was around eight o'clock in the morning. The grass tops were still watery. Namaga folded up the lower part of his trousers so that they would not get wet. The two walked towards the oak-tree crushing the dew under their feet.

'Who do you suspect of the crime?' asked Namaga.

'Nobody, sir. As my wife said this morning the hut could have burnt by itself. Accidents happen like that, sir.'

'But that would be impossible, because the criminal dug under the beam of my hut and took away my two hundred dollars in addition. Your wife must have forgotten about that.'

'You are right sir, but I don't suspect anyone although people have their eyes fixed on Beshir.'

'That's the man I suspect, too,' said Namaga.

There were a few people sitting on the protruding roots of the oak tree. A red cloth was swaying from one of the branches of the oak tree, on which a rook sat, busy pecking at what initially appeared to be worms, but which Namaga discovered to be greasy food-remains instead. The pagan section of the population still worshipped the oak tree and during the Maskal week they tied to its branches coloured cloths and beads. They also smeared it with butter and poured a jar of locally brewed beer over it. The Christians and the Moslems of course laughed at such bygone customs and took away the cloths and beads without being seen by the pagans.

[84]

After a short while the sub-district governor and the Cheka Shum arrived, followed by a few dozen peasants, and the place was full of people as in the previous meetings. The elders went away to conduct the Afersata while the rest of the crowd waited under the tree. 'In your report you mentioned that you lost two hundred dollars,' said the sub-district governor eyeing Namaga, 'but you didn't tell us the details of it. How did you lose it?'

'Well, I just lost it the night my hut burnt down.'

'But how?'

'Well, I believe it was stolen.'

'It could have burnt together with the hut or wasn't that possible?'

'That couldn't possibly be the case, sir. I bu . . . .'

He almost said 'I buried it in the ground.' But he felt ashamed, and on second thought he said, 'the criminal must have carried it away, sir.'

'But your boxes were rescued. And if you put the money in one of your boxes, then it must have been rescued too.'

'It was not in any of the boxes, sir. I put it in a safer place.'

The crowd was interested in the exchange of words between the sub-district governor and Namaga. Those who were sitting way back came forward. Those who were nearby cleaned their ears with their little fingers in order to follow better the questions and answers.

'Perhaps you put it in one of the sacks together with your coffee grains,' said the governor.

'No, sir. It was in a much safer place. But the thief took it away.'

'You must give us proof that it was stolen. Otherwise you cannot get compensation for it.'

'Did anybody know about your stolen money, except yourself?' intervened the Cheka Shum.

'I am a respectable person in this village, sir, I have never lied about such matters,' he said, looking with appealing eyes towards the sub-district governor.

'Of course. Of course. There is no doubt about that. But still there must be proof that you lost the money on that particular night,' went on the Cheka Shum, 'and I am pretty sure that there is at least one person who knew about your money.'

'Well indeed there is one person who knew about it.'

'And who is that person?'

'My wife knew about it.'

'She also knew exactly where you put the money?'

'That has no importance, sir. I just put it away in a safe place, and it disappeared.'

'He must have buried it in the ground!' said a voice among the crowd.

Namaga felt a shock running down his spinal chord as the crowd roared with laughter.

'Who just said that I buried it in the ground?' shouted back Namaga with anger.

Silence followed. Then Beshir rose up and said, 'What the miser stored away, the white ants ate away. I am the one who said you must have buried it in the ground.'

'That is right, sir. I did bury it in the ground. But . . . .' There was another burst of laughter that drowned the words of Namaga. 'But how does Beshir know that I buried it in the ground? Only the man who stole away my money could have known about it.'

There was dead silence once again. The implication of Namaga's words pricked Beshir like a needle. 'I just supposed, knowing that you are a tight-fisted fellow, that you must have buried it in the ground. Otherwise why didn't you want to tell us where you hid it?' said Beshir.

'Mela!' called out the village headman at this instant, 'you are wanted by the elders. Go and give your words.'

'Did you set alight Namaga's hut?' asked the elders.

'No. I didn't,' answered Mela.

'Have you seen the man who set it alight?'

'No, I haven't.'

'Have you heard of the man who did it?'

'Yes,' he said, 'people say Beshir did it.'

'Who are the people who say that?'

'Well, everybody suspects Beshir. And even Namaga is having a hot argument with him at this very moment.'

'But do you suspect him of the crime?'

'Yes, like everyone else.'

'Why do you suspect him?'

'Well, he previously killed two goats that he had stolen from his uncles. And he has been suspected of such crimes for a long time now.'

'Do you have any evidence to suspect him of burning Namaga's hut?'

'Nothing more that what I just told you.'

'Then put out this fire swearing on the life of your offspring.' Mela swore.

'Wipe off the ashes, swearing once again.' Mela did what he was told to do.

The crowd was noisy when the elders closed the case and came back to the oak tree to give the final report of their investigation. Some of the villagers were more or less sure that the elders would condemn Beshir. Others were worried for themselves, for how many times the unexpected happens in such investigations! 'Silence!' shouted the Cheka Shum, 'Sit down everybody. The report is to be given.' The elders also sat down, except the one with the longest grey beard who went to the governor to whisper something in his ear. Then standing in the centre of the crowd he started to give the report orally, in the following words:

'May the tongue tell truth. May God give issue to those who have none. May the young ones grow up to be adults. May the adults live long to be elders and to be wise. May the bright day give place to a peaceful night.'

'Fellow villagers,' the elder went on, 'it is already a few months since we started this investigation. Our villages have become a hiding place for thieves, and for other criminals. More huts will be burnt, more animals and more money will be stolen in the future, if we don't co-operate in indicating the criminal with our forefingers, without fear. In this particular case, that is in the affair of Namaga's hut, I regret to inform you that we have totally failed.'

'Is he going to suggest another Afersata for this same matter? Or else what is he going to do?' whispered the villagers in each other's ears. But the elder with the longest grey beard went on, 'Fellow villagers, we are all responsible for the burning of Namaga's hut, and we are all condemned collectively to compensate him for his loss, because we have failed to find out the criminal. There could, of course, be another Afersata, and another, and still another on this same affair. But of what use will that be? If anyone had knowledge of the criminal and the courage to expose him he would have done so by now. But as yet nobody has given us evidence to that effect. In the circumstances we have only one course of action to take. And that is to condemn ourselves to pay the expenses of Namaga. I give you this report on behalf of the seven elders you have elected to investigate the crime.'

To finish the formalities the sub-district governor rose up from his seat when the bearded elder sat down, and asked the crowd: 'Do you agree to the judgment of the elders?'

'Yes we do,' came out the unanimous voice of the crowd.

'Do you?'

'Yes, we do.'

'Do you?'

'Yes, we do.'

After three shouts of, 'yes, we do,' the case of the burnt hut was irrevocably closed. The next step was for the Cheka Shum and his assistants to go from hearth to hearth and collect the sum due from each peasant.